This book belongs to

....

The Elves and the Shoemaker

Key sound s-blends spellings:
sc, scr, sk, sl, sn, sp, spl, spr, squ, st, str, sw

Secondary sounds: oi, st (ending)

Written by Rosie Greening
Illustrated by Clare Fennell

Reading with phonics

How to use this book

The **Reading with phonics** series helps you to have fun with your child and to support their learning of phonics and reading. It is aimed at children who have learned the letter sounds and are building confidence in their reading.

Each title in the series focuses on a different key sound or blend of sounds. The entertaining retelling of the story repeats this sound frequently, and the different spellings for the sound or blend of sounds are highlighted in red type. The first activity at the back of the book provides practice in reading and using words containing the sound. This title looks at a key consonant blend group, where two or more consonants are blended together, but each sound may be heard in the blend. The key group of consonant blends for **The Elves and the Shoemaker** is the *s-blend*.

Start by reading the story to your child, asking them to join in with the refrain in bold. Next, encourage them to read the story with you. Give them a hand to decode tricky words.

Now look at the activity pages at the back of the book. These are intended for you and your child to enjoy together. Most are not activities to complete in pencil or pen, but by reading and talking or pointing.

The **Key sound** pages focus on one sound or on a group of consonant blends. Encourage your child to read the different letter groups and complete the activity, so they become more aware of the variety of spellings there are for the same sound or for the group of consonant blends.

The **Letters together** pages look at pairs or groups of letters and at the sounds they make as they work together. Help your child to read the words and trace the route on the word maps.

Rhyme is used a lot in these retellings. Whatever stage your child has reached in their learning of phonics, it is always good practice for them to listen carefully for sounds and find words that rhyme. The pages on **Rhyming words** take six words from the story and ask children to read and find other words that rhyme with them.

The **Key words** pages focus on a number of key words that occur regularly but can nonetheless be challenging. Many of these words are not sounded out following the rules of phonics and the easiest thing is for children to learn them by sight, so that they do not worry about decoding them. These pages encourage children to retell the story, practising key words as they do so.

The **Picture dictionary** page asks children to focus closely on nine words from the story. Encourage children to look carefully at each word, cover it with their hand, write it on a separate piece of paper, and finally, check it!

Do not complete all the activities at once – doing one each time you read will ensure that your child continues to enjoy the stories and the time you are spending together. **Have fun!**

Scott stitched strong and sturdy shoes
to try and sell each day.
Each style was plain and simple,
in a choice of brown or grey.

But no one ever bought the shoes,
which meant that Scott was poor.
They'd shout, "Your shoes are boring!"
And then storm out of his store!

Scott has got a simple store.
The shoes don't sell, so Scott stays poor.

It wasn't long until Scott had
just three more coins to use.
He spent them on some leather
to make one last pair of shoes.

He spread the leather out to start,
but longed to sleep instead.
He put his scruffy slippers on,
then scurried straight to bed.

Scott has got a simple store.
He spends his coins and has no more!

When Scott awoke, he got a scare:
the leather had all gone.
But then he stared, for in its place,
two sparkly shoes now shone!

The shoes were truly stunning,
so he put them on display.
A woman quickly spotted them
and sprinted in to say . . .

Scott has got a simple store.
A woman speeds in through the door.

"I'd like to buy those stylish shoes;
they're splendid as can be."
She handed Scott some coins and squealed,
"Please stitch more shoes for me."

Thought Scott, "This is a stroke of luck;
and what have I to lose?
If I buy leather with these coins,
perhaps I'll find more shoes."

Scott has got a simple store.
This deal's too perfect to ignore!

When Scott woke up, two pairs of shoes
were standing in his store.
He put them on the special shelf,
just like he'd done before.

Again, the woman scurried in
and said, "I'll take both pairs!"
Then off she skipped to spread the word
about Scott's splendid wares.

Scott has got a simple store.
The woman's sure to buy some more!

Her story spread, and soon the store
was featured in the news.
And from then on, the people swarmed
to buy Scott's swanky shoes!

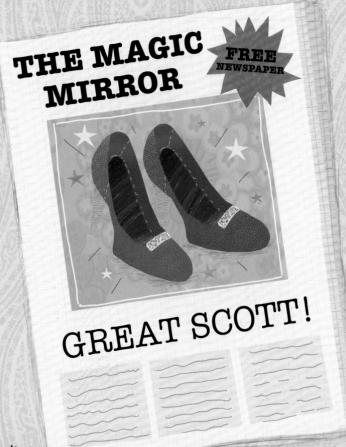

THE MAGIC
MIRROR

FREE
NEWSPAPER

GREAT SCOTT!

One morning, Scott woke up and thought,
"I'm rich as I could be.
I only wish that I could know
who makes these shoes for me."

Scott has got a swanky store.
And now he's richer than before!

So Scott spread lots of leather out,
and hid behind a door.
And soon two scruffy elves snuck in
and sprung across the floor.

They scrambled up the table legs
in old and tattered suits,
then stitched with skill until they'd made
some snazzy leather boots!

Scott has got a super store.
The skilful elves make shoes galore!

As soon as all the work was done,
they sped off like a shot.
"I must repay the elves!" Scott thought,
and stayed up late to plot.

Before too long, Scott had a plan
to thank the helpful pair.
He stitched some special, stylish suits
and shoes for them to wear.

Scott has got a special store.
He stitches suits they'll both adore!

That night, the elves came by again
and spied the splendid clothes.
They tried each outfit on with joy,
then stopped to strike a pose!

The elves were so excited
that they asked if they could stay.
They moved into Scott's store at once,
and made new shoes each day!

Scott has got a special store.
The elves look stylish, that's for sure!

Thanks to the elves, Scott always had
great stacks of shoes to sell.
And since Scott's clothes had been a hit,
the store stocked suits as well!

Scott has got a special store.
The elves will stay forever more!

SCOTT'S
SHOES
'N' SUITS

CLOSED

23

Key sound

The s-blends are sc, scr, sk, sl, sn, sp, spl, spr, squ, st, str and sw. Practise these sounds by looking at the words in the pictures and using them to make sentences. Can you use each word in a different sentence?

slippers sleep

Scott
scare

spread
sprinted

squeal
square

skipped
skill

special
sparkly

snazzy

straight
strong

swarmed

style
store

splendid

scruffy
scrambled

Letters together

Look at these pairs of letters and say the sounds they make.

oi **st**

Follow the words containing oi to find some coins.

oi

oil

door

boot

join

hid

choice

coins

skill

noise

Follow the words containing st at the end to find the best shoe.

brown

st ···· simple

woman

fast

last ········ must

sell

just

three

best

SCOTT'S
SHOES
'N' SUITS

27

Rhyming words

Read and say the words in the
flowers and point to other
words that rhyme with them.

pair	**stare**	bed
there		pennies

just	**must**	trust
old		thank

store	**snore**	shoe
poor		more

grow	last	sew
fast		past

will	skill	hill
shelf		news

poor	strong	song
wrong		pair

Now choose a word and make up a rhyming chant!

In the **store**, Scott starts to **snore**.

29

Key words

Many common words can be tricky to sound out. Practise them by reading these sentences about the story. Now make more sentences using other key words from around the border.

Scott **made** plain and simple shoes.

No one bought the shoes, **so** Scott was poor.

Scott put out **some** leather and went to bed.

When he woke up, he found some sparkly shoes!

something · some · big · it

· couldn't · little · a · her · had · that · day · the · we

A woman **saw** the shoes and bought them.

That night, more shoes appeared.

Scott sold the shoes and got **very** rich.

Scott saw two elves making **the** shoes.

He made **little** suits for the elves.

From **then** on, Scott and the elves worked together.

by · saw · and · help · house · the · called · when · on · because · up · you · they

old · there · made · into · so · then · took · very

Picture dictionary

Look carefully at the pictures and the words.
Now cover the words, one at a time.
Can you remember how to write them?

boots

coins

elves

leather

news

shoe

store

suit

woman